Dear Parent:
Your child's love of reading starts here!

Every child learns to read in a different way and at his or her own speed. Some go back and forth between reading levels and read favorite books again and again. Others read through each level in order. You can help your young reader improve and become more confident by encouraging his or her own interests and abilities. From books your child reads with you to the first books he or she reads alone, there are I Can Read Books for every stage of reading:

SHARED READING
Basic language, word repetition, and whimsical illustrations, ideal for sharing with your emergent reader

BEGINNING READING
Short sentences, familiar words, and simple concepts for children eager to read on their own

READING WITH HELP
Engaging stories, longer sentences, and language play for developing readers

READING ALONE
Complex plots, challenging vocabulary, and high-interest topics for the independent reader

I Can Read Books have introduced children to the joy of reading since 1957. Featuring award-winning authors and illustrators and a fabulous cast of beloved characters, I Can Read Books set the standard for beginning readers.

A lifetime of discovery begins with the magical words "I Can Read!"

Visit www.icanread.com for information
on enriching your child's reading experience.

I Can Read® and I Can Read Book® are trademarks of HarperCollins Publishers.

Based on characters from *The Elf on the Shelf: A Christmas Tradition* by
Carol V. Aebersold and Chanda A. Bell © 2005

The Elf on the Shelf: Meet the Scout Elves

® / T M / © 2023 CCA and B, LLC d/b/a The Lumistella Company. All rights reserved.

Printed in the United States of America.
For information address HarperCollins Children's Books, a division of HarperCollins Publishers,
195 Broadway, New York, NY 10007.
www.icanread.com

ISBN 978-0-06-332739-9

Book design by John Sazaklis

23 24 25 26 27 LB 10 9 8 7 6 5 4 3 2 1   First Edition

I Can Read!

the ELF on the SHELF®
a Christmas tradition ™

Meet the Scout Elves

Adapted by Alexandra West

HARPER
An Imprint of HarperCollinsPublishers

WELCOME

Welcome to the North Pole!
The North Pole is a magical place
where Santa and his elves live.
But these are no ordinary elves!

These are Scout Elves!

Scout Elves have many different skills.

They are great candy painters and

speedy mailroom sorters.

Scout Elves are terrific
toy testers, too!

But their biggest job
is being reporting Scout Elves!

Reporting Scout Elves
are very important.
They are Santa's most
trusted helpers.

Each Scout Elf is assigned
to a family.
Every year, Scout Elves
fly across the world.
They can't wait to see you!

Reporting Scout Elves
love to share fun and good cheer.
They wear pointy hats and red suits
with white collars.
Some elves wear
funny costumes too!

11

Each day,

Scout Elves find a spot

in their family's home.

They love to play

hide-and-seek!

Your elf could be anywhere.

It could be on a shelf

or even in your stocking!

Each night,

Scout Elves fly back

to the North Pole.

They tell Santa

all the nice things you've done.

This helps Santa make

his Nice List!

When elves are on the job,
they become very still.
Scout Elves can only move
when you are not looking.
They are good listeners,
but can't talk to you.
This is what makes them
such good helpers
for Santa.

Scout Elves have many

other talents as well.

A good Scout Elf
can hide and sneak
behind presents!

No two Scout Elves are the same.

They each have different names

and personalities!

What's your elf's name?

Is it Snowflake or Sprinkles?

Maybe it's Blink?

It could even be Popsicle!

These elves waste no time
making themselves at home.
You may notice that
in the morning your elf
has not moved.

Do not panic!
Scout Elves will sometimes
return to their favorite
spot in the house.
Make sure to
check on them
later in the day.

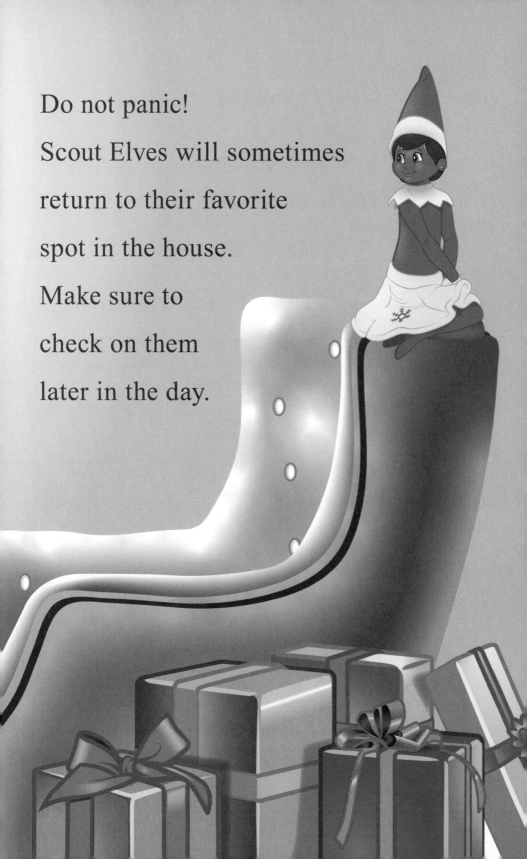

Be sure to treat your elf kindly.

If Scout Elves are

accidentally touched,

they may lose their magic.

Not to worry!

There are three ways you can
restore a Scout Elf's magic.
First, write a note to say "Sorry!"

Second, sprinkle a little cinnamon
near your elf.

Cinnamon is like a vitamin for elves.

It will help them regain their magic.

Third, elves love Christmas carols.

Try singing one with your family!

Then comes the big day.

It's Christmas morning!

Santa left you presents!

Your elf must have done a great job
telling Santa how good you were.

Every reporting Scout Elf
loves Christmas Day.
They return to the North Pole
for a big celebration.
Elves will celebrate a job well done
by playing in the powdery snow.

Oh, what fun!

See you next year!

Merry Christmas!